You Don't Know Me

by rainbo b. seed

Book 3
When You Live
To Fly

What critics are saying about this amazing magical-realism series for teens and young adults:

"The most original adventure series since Harry Potter!"

"A magical journey along the border of fantasy and reality."

"A must read!"

"Hilarious and heart-warming!"

"There has never been a heroine like Rainbo B. Seed!"

The You Don't Know Me series follows Rainbo, a rebellious heroine, who has special powers to speak to the reptilian realm, and sees spectacular visions in her dreams. Rainbo is strong-willed, funny, resourceful, and quick thinking, and committed to fighting the injustices of the world.

Each book in the series offers a humorous and wise lesson along life's magical journey.

When You Live To Fly is a beautiful, magical-realistic story about aspiration and inspiration as Rainbo and the Snake Clan rewrite the ancient Oracle of "No Flying" to the endearing "Live To Fly".

Join Rainbo as she teaches a corps of snakes how fly and twirl, and creates a show that becomes so popular huge crowds come from near and far to see it. Her popularity grows into a national phenomenon until she is offered an audition on "America's Got Talent".

Along the way, her grandmother communes with the Snake Elders, discovers a cure for her 'forgetfulness disease', and transforms into a "Snakewoman Curandera"; Rainbo encounters Billy and learns about his "curse of fragmentation", and his special gift; and faces one challenge after another before she learns a life lesson that only the Snake Clan can teach her.

Rainbo's perserverance, strength, and inquisitive nature, make her into a unique heroine who faces life with humor and resilience, and learns what it means to believe in your own aspirations above all else.

Other Spectacular Books
In The <u>You Don't Know Me</u> Series
Book One
<u>When The Stars Call Your Name</u>

Experience Rainbo's hilarious trials and tribulations as she discovers her special gift of communicating with the subterranean world of reptiles, becomes best friends with a member of the notorious "snake clan", outsmarts the F.B.I. and learns the deep wisdom of the "stars calling her name" in this wild and original new series.

Book Two
<u>When You Put Your Head</u>
<u>In A Crocodile's Mouth</u>

In this truly magical story, Rainbo heroically leaps onto a ravenous crocodile to save the Natureland Park's Director Mr. I. Q. Dangerous, stands up to the bullying Bad Boyz Gang, discovers the secret of her grandmother's "forgetfulness" disease, studies ancient Native American spells and potions, and stops the evil "Protective Services" from taking her grandmother away from her and her mother.

Book Three
When You Live To Fly

Here is a tale of spectacular joy and rollicking fun as we learn the difference between the ancient oracles of "No Flying" versus "Live To Fly".

Follow Rainbo as she teaches a corp of snakes to fly in Rainbo's "School For Twirlers and Flyers", attracts huge crowds from near and far to see her show, gets chosen to be on "America's Got Talent", and cures her grandmother's "forgetfulness disease". "A wonderful tale of aspiration and revelation!"

Book Four
When Your Power Animal
Speaks To You

Imagine Rainbo running away deep into the forest after she witnesses a murder. Her only friends are an owl who speaks in riddles and a snake that is afraid of the dark. She is hungry and alone and can't find her way back home. What will happen? Are the murderers still looking for her? Will her mother and friends find her before the killers?

"A truly exciting tale of perserverance, ingenuity, and wisdom!" "I loved every page!"

Book Five
<u>When You Are On</u>
<u>A Vision Quest</u>

Rainbo discovers her power animal and learns her journey in the forest is a vision quest to realize her meaning and special purpose. Her spiritual and physical journey empowers her to face the killers who have been chasing her and accept her heroic nature.

"Another fabulous tale in this original series that offers readers a lasting message and beautiful ending!"

Please visit our websites to discover special offers or to contact the author:

newworldpublishers.com
rainbosblog.com
rainbobseed.com

You Don't Know Me
Book Three: When You Live To Fly
Copyright © 2019 by r g cantalupo (aka rainbo b. seed)

ISBN 978-1-7332883-5-4

Published in USA by New World Publishers
www.newworldpublishers.com

When You Live to Fly

How It All Began

"What do you see, child?"

"Looks like one of Slim's sons," I said and pointed out the black body slithering across our yard.

"Maybe he's coming to tell you something."

"If he comin' to tell me somethin', why's he tryin' to slip away shy as a ghost."

"Ghosts aren't so shy as you imagine, Rainbo. Sometimes ghosts have so much to say they can hardly keep it all in. That's why they blow out candles and open up window shutters and make sounds like an old woman moaning because they are trying to get someone to pay attention to what they need to say. No, snakes and ghosts don't appear without a reason."

I knowed she was right.

But I didn't think being ghost-like was a message I

could decipher just then, so I got up and cut off the path where the snake was headed and stood in front of him waitin' for him to come.

When he reached the shadow of my feet, he tried to dart off in another direction, but I was two steps ahead of him.

I snatched him up and looked him in the eyes.

"What you tryin' to escape from little fella? I ain't gonna hurt you. You Slim's son, ain't you?"

Well, maybe he was there for a reason and maybe he weren't. He sure didn't seem like he was. He couldn't hardly whisper right from bein' so scared and discombobulated and probably never heard a human snake-whisper before.

"What's your name, son?"

"Sssss-slll-i-i-i-mmm."

If you never heard a snake stutter 'fore you got a sure rib-tickle comin', 'cause it's hard 'enuff hearin' a snake whisperin' bein' as how their throats so long and the sound has to carry through such a windin' tunnel of snake-flesh, but when that low sound is magnified by a stutter why you just as soon put your ear 'gainst their mouth and guess what words comin' out rather than try to decipher them suspiratin' sounds from a distance.

"Sssss-slll-i-i-i-mmmzzz-mmmm-my-my pop-my pop-my pa-pa.   I-I-I-I'm-his...dau...dau...daughter. Ec...ho."

"Echo. Well, if that ain't a perfect match. So what you doin' here, Echo?"

"Wh-wh-where's here?"

"In my yard."

"I-I-I'm-lost."

"You ain't lost, you're just discombobulated. Your home is over there past that vacant field."

"I-I-I'm far-si-si-sighted. I ca-ca-can't see m-m-more than a f-f-few f-f-feet in f-f-front of me. R-r-runs in the f-f-family."

"I know."

Now I still didn't know the meaning of her being here and maybe there weren't none 'cept her farsightedness and bein lost and all but I figured she weren't getting' home no how less I took her.

"Grandma will you be alright while I take's Echo home?"

"What do you think, child'? You think I want to sit here watching them buffalo grazing while you are off having an adventure with the snake family?

13

Why don't you show me where Slim and his family live?"

And with that, we walked toward the back of our yard and crossed a vacant field and followed a short path to a great big oak tree that had hearts and arrows and lovers' names and initials engraved all over its trunk. There was a round knothole 'bout the size of a softball in the middle of the trunk and that's where Slim and his family lived.

"Here you go, Echo," and I dropped her into the knothole.

"My, my, my," said grandma, "I should've guessed this would be their home."

"Why you say that, grandma?"

"Because this is where it all started."

"Where what all started?"

"Before your mama was born, before even this city was born

and there was just farms and orchards where these streets are now, your granddaddy and I met here at this same tree."

"Granddaddy Lou, the baseball player." I'd heard 'bout my grand-father, even seen a handsome picture of him posed all manly in his uniform, but he'd passed on before I come into this world.

"Sweet Lou Silver, "The Cobra" they called him because of the way he pitched with that jerky cobralike delivery that fooled everyone. He was the best pitcher in the negro leagues, he and a fella named Sachel. I lived in the church across the street. All the Timicuan, Sioux, and Lakota girls lived in church schools until they turned eighteen in those days. The government called it an assimilation program, wanted us to learn

English, blend into the culture, adapt to the white ways. They wanted us to become Christians, forget the Great Spirit, and give up our rituals and beliefs so that we could be saved and go to heaven. We went along with it, most anyway, pretended to believe what they wanted us to believe so we wouldn't be punished, spend the night in solitary, or do extra work as penance. The baseball field was over there, across that road."

"Where those apartments are?"

"Yes, about there. Green Field they called it, because it was so green the baseballs got green grass stains on them and after awhile turned green as an emerald from playing there."

"So we girls used to watch the games from the second story windows of the barracks and there was your grandfather, this long, dark, drink of water that was tall and handsome as nobody's business. First time I saw him my heart fluttered like one of those newborn butterflies floating on the wind."

"And before long, I'm sneaking out at night to meet him. He never met a Timicuan girl before, or even First Peoples for that matter, and I never met a Negro man before, but from the first time we sat down and looked long and deep into each other's eyes we knew we were going to spend the rest of our lives together. That's our initials there, in the center."

"The ones inside the heart, grandma?"

"Yes, that's the first heart and the first love letters ever written on that tree."

I'd never seen my grandma cry. Even when she was sad as a

blue moon, even when her arthritis ached somethin' fierce or bad luck had beaten her down to dust, she'd put a smile over that sadness and let on that there was nothin' wrong. But when she looked at them initials and that old weather-beaten heart carved in the trunk, well, the truth of her love and that time gone by was just too much for her. Tears slid down her high cheekbones and washed through the deep furrows of her face.

She was silent for a long, long time.

And then, little by little, she woke from her memory-dream.

"Goes by so fast, Rainbo. So fast. And yet, when I look at that heart, it seems like we were just here. Here. Yesterday. The buffalo grazing and the mustangs galloping free and Bear- Running- Up- The-

Mountain leading us through the pass, and Sweet Lou and your mother's laughing newborn face."

"But they're gone, and you know they're gone, gone like a leaf blowing by, or a bird gliding on the current, or a dream you can't remember whole.

"And then a day comes when the Great Spirit calls you and you go Rainbo, you go and you meet Her, and you rejoin those faces and those half-remembered dreams and then the circle is complete."

I didn't know exactly what she meant 'bout the circle of life and the Great Spirit callin' you, but I knew it was somethin' like the night I learned to hear the silence and so the meanin' would someday come to me.

Grandma showed me the heart and the initials of her and

my granddaddy carved on that oak for all eternity and though I didn't know how Slim and his family and my granddaddy "The Cobra" was all connected, I knew somewhere it all was woven together like one of them blankets grandma made where all the patterns came together but there was still one knot left undone, unfinished so that the cycle of life went on and on and the connections was never complete 'cause the cosmos was ever-changin', and always needed to ever-change.

Well, seemed like forever passed in that moment with grandma and I lookin' at that heart carved in the center of the tree, and then, suddenly, a head popped out of the knothole and then more heads popped out and soon the whole knothole was filled with snakeheads from Slim and his family.

Now you can't imagine all the commotion when a clan of snakes gets to whisperin'.

Sounds like an avalanche of fallen leaves rollin' down a hillside.

Sounds like a sixteen-wheeled truck comin' down the highway.

Sounds like...

Well, you gets the notion.

And then Slim slithers out and crawls up my arm and soon the whole clan is twisted round my arms and legs and neck like bracelets and necklaces and anklets and leglets and armlets like some kind of exotic African

21

jewelry. I even had three or four of the younger snakes climb up my head and wrap round my red-haired Afro like they was a turbin.

"Why, Rainbo, don't you look the sight? You look like a snake-charmer, or a gypsy dancer," laughed grandma.

Now I ain't one for all that hallelujah glory for doin' somethin' I loved, but it did make me happy seein' my grandma smile, and have her mind come back from the past, and not be feelin' them arthritic aches and reminisin' pains.

And it made me feel good not to have to fret 'bout her wanderin' off somewhere, or watchin' her stare out into the turquoise sky like she was seein' her whole life pass by in the clouds.

So, yeah, I was happy.

I was happy my grandma was here with me and she and Slim and Junior and Echo and Sweet Lou and the tree with the lovers' voices and the knothole was here and we was all gathered for the moment, and out of my gladness and excitement I pulled Slim from 'round my neck and threw him high up in the air like I was some kind of cheerleader and Slim was a black and yellow pom pom. I hurled Slim so high up in the air from my excitement and my happiness that he went above the crown of that old oak tree and two blue jays stopped mid-air to gaze at this twistin' and twirlin' bird flyin' through the sky. Then, when he reached as high as he could go, he just fell like a shootin' star, fallin' down so fast he looked like a fuzzy blur of color, droppin' straight down from where I threw him, and I was gettin' ready to catch him and every body was waitin' for him to come down and he was whirlin' and twirlin' and then suddenly he dropped into my hands and everybody gasped from the wild adrenalin of the twirlin' whirlin' feat.

Everyone was struck frozen with their mouths gapin' and their eyes bugged out like they'd seen a miracle or somethin'.

Even grandma, who seen more'n her share of miracles, just stood there with her mouth wide open lookin' at that place in the sky where I'd hurled Slim up and caught him again.

And then everyone just seemed to unfreeze all at once and started jabberin' and there was such a gag-gle of voices I couldn't hardly make out nothin' 'cept everyone was lookin' at me like I was some kind of wizard.

And what they wanted more than anything was to see that magical twirlin' feat done again.

Grandma's eyes were so lit up and sparklin' I'd have thought she'd come face to face with the Great Spirit herself and She done told her she was gonna be a red-tailed hawk in the life after.

"Child, you have more gifts than I ever imagined. You have the gifts of the Great Shaman from long ago."

Well, to make a short story long, one by one I hurled Slim and Echo and Junior and his brothers and sisters and a dozen or so other relatives up in the air that afternoon, whirlin' and twirlin' that snake family high above that ole' oak tree, and I watched grandma's eyes sparkle and flash and that permanent smile slide over her face, and sometimes I didn't catch them right, and sometimes they bounced off of my head and plopped onto my shoulder, and sometimes they caught a hold of my neck or arm or leg, and some even bounced off me and bounced onto grandma, and some bounced off of me and then bounced off grandma and then fell onto the grass, and I don't think there was ever such a happy union of strange characters, and odd happen-ings, since the first big-headed, green-skinned aliens done met up with the Neanderthal clan.

Every now and then a snake would twist his or her body this

way or that to try and control their balance in the currents.

And some would catch a little wave of air and ride a ways, and some would twirl out over the tree-tops and then come back.

And, by the end of the day, there was only a small leap of faith between the twirlin' and the flyin', but that leap of faith hadn't happen-ed yet.

As the days went by, me and Slim and the snake family got so good at the snake-twirlin', people started comin' from miles around to watch us.

Wasn't a lot at first.

Just a few kids from my school showin' up.

But each day, a few more

came.

Then a mother or a father came with their kids.

And then whole families came, and 'fore long the vacant lot was filled with crowds of people and dogs and cats and forest creatures all screamin' and yellin' and clap-pin' for more.

And, as the crowds got bigger, and we got better, the snake-twirlin' feats got more and more specta-cular.

First, I had one snake, then two, then three snakes twirlin' simultan-eous in the air.

Then, I learned to catch snakes from behind my back, and between my legs, and upside down while doin' a headstand.

Then, I learned to do cartwheels, and splits, and crab walks, and balance one snake on my head while two was spinnin' in the air.

And as I was learnin' more excitin' tricks, the snakes was learnin' more and more excitin' twirls and swirls.

But The Flyin',

...well, that happened by accident.

I was twirlin' Junior up and catchin' him on the other side of the oak and Junior would do his four-and-a-half twists-with-a-full-spiral, (which was his special trick), and I would catch him behind my back.

And it just so happened this was a particularly windy day, and Junior weren't just any snake: he was a genius of the air.

(Junior could do more twirlin' and swirlin' tricks than any snake had a mind to. He was doin' four twirls and a swirl while the rest of the snake clan was still tryin' to do three twirls and a half-swirl.)

What no one knowed though, was that Junior had been studyin' the birds. He'd climbed

31

up to the top of the oak tree and crawled to the edge of a branch and studied the hawks and the ravens and the whippoorwills as they floated on the currents and how they caught the wind in their feathers so they could hover mid-air.

If'n he could shape himself like a wing, Junior imagined, he could catch a current too, maybe even glide and hover and float on the waves of wind.

So, when I threw Junior up, he was still imaginin' hawks flyin', and suddenly, halfway through his ascent, (when he's supposed to be doin' the twirlin' and swirlin' tricks), he flattens his body out thin as a flapjack.

Now he ain't goin' up over the crown of the tree and then twirlin' back down to my hand.

No, he's shootin' up high over the oak and disappearin' in the clouds.

Well, I'm just standin' there lookin' up, searchin' the white-cotton cumulus tryin' to find his black speck somewhere in the clouds, wonderin' how I'm ever gonna catch him when I can't even find him in the sky.

See, there was one rule I learned early on 'bout snake-twirlin: It wasn't the goin' up that was hard; it was the comin' down.

In all the snake-twirlin' I'd done up to that moment, I'd never had a serious accident.

Oh, I'd had a few lumps on my head from an unexpected wind causin' a miscalculation.
I'd gotten bruises on my shoulders and arms for missin' a

catch or from a snake fallin' hard in the wrong direction.

Every now and then a snake got knocked unconscious from a crash landin', and ended with a headache or a sore muscle or a bruise on his tail, but I never missed a catch completely, and no snake I ever tossed up into the sky ever fell back to earth without me first breakin' his fall.

But Junior's flight was different.

He'd flattened his body out and caught a current and was flyin' higher than anyone knowed a snake could fly.

And it weren't like he was flyin' straight up and comin' straight back down.

No, once he caught that current, he was ridin' the waves through the clouds.

He weren't headin' toward the other side of the oak where I was supposed to catch him, he was headin' toward the apartments and the highway and the city's tall buildings.

If he came down somewhere in the heart of the city...well, I didn't want to think what would become of him.

Wouldn't be me or a tree branch or a mound of leaves to break his fall.

Wouldn't be nothin' but the hard concrete, or the black asphalt for his body to crash into.

Well, I didn't want to imagine the consequences so I got's to runnin' and runnin' tryin' hard to stay beneath him.

I ran through foxtails and dog-weed and sage brush.

I ran through thorny rose bushes and over white picket fences and through backyard junkyards.

I ran and ran and ran and after awhile I didn't have no idea where I'd run to.

And up above me was Junior ridin' the currents like he was surfin' clouds.
And there was cars shootin' by around me and people yellin' and car horns honkin' and nobody had a clue what I was chasin' or if some-thin' was chasin' me.

And then the strangest thing happened.

Junior turned his body 'round, and instead of headin' toward the heart of the city, now he was headin' back toward the heart of the woods.

So I did my own twist n' twirl, and spun round with him...and ran and ran and ran...

Junior slowly descended, comin' lower and lower, twirlin' round and around like one of those helicopter whirligigs, as he slowed himself down!

Yes sirree, Junior was descendin' from the clouds, and he was con-trollin' his speed and his direction and contortin' his body into all kinda shapes to catch the wind, and suddenly I realized: Junior wasn't just glidin' on the currents, he wasn't just goin' up and down ridin' on the waves of wind, he was actually flyin'!

Flyin'!

Well, I decided right then and there there was more mysteries in the world then I'd ever have a mind to fathom so I best just stand where I was and let the Great Spirit guide Junior back into my hands.

So I stopped runnin'.

And I stopped lookin' up at the clouds tryin' to keep track of where he was.

I looked 'round me to get my bearings back.
And guess where I was?

Right smack dab in the center of the field where I started.

Right in front of that ole' oak tree with grandma lookin' at me like I was a Shaman or someone.

She was standin' there waitin', and Slim was there, and the whole rest of the Snake Clan was there, and there was a whole congregation of people and creatures gathered in the field as well, waitin' for Junior to land.

There was squirrels, and blue jays, and rabbits, and deer, and there was preying mantises, and butterflies, and grasshoppers, and a whole cornucopia of crawlin', and flyin,' and hoppin', insects...

And there was kids from my school and parents and teachers and a motley crowd of who-knows-who- strangers...

And they was all standin' round waitin', watchin' the sky, followin' Junior's swirlin' whirlygig-twirls as he kept comin' down, down, down.

And Junior had a smile on his face, swirlin' and twirlin' and spinnin', catchin' the wind in the sail of his bowed body as he whirlygiged down.

Then, at the very, very last possible moment, he turns his flattened body out like a sideways flapjack, catches the wind to slow down even more, and floats gentle as a feather into my palms.

It was the most excitin', death-defyin' feat of aeronautical exper-tise any of us had ever seen.

The crowd was stone quiet.

I was stone still.

Then, a loud roar rose up out of the silence and a tremendous cheer echoed through the woods.

Junior was a hero, he'd survived his spectacular, maiden flight.

Finally, someone put me up on their shoulders and carried me and Junior 'round the crowd.

Creatures were clappin' and cheerin' and yowlin' and makin' such a commotion I thought the whole city of Oakville was gonna descend on us to see what was goin' on.

When the crowd finally let us down, Junior was asked how he'd learned to fly.

He explained that he had studied the hawks, and the ravens, and the owls, and had done exercises to prepare his body to stretch this way and that, and to flatten out, and bow like a sail and so forth, and when the current was right, he'd caught it, and tried to make his body into a wing like the birds he'd seen.

After Junior's explanation, there was another great roar from the crowd and creatures started chant-in' "Flyer! Flyer! Flyer!"

And then Junior was whisked off on top of someone else's shoulders and I was left standin' there with grandma.

I still didn't understand how Junior had done it really.

I guessed it showed, 'cause grandma saw the question and worry in my face, and tried to give me an answer.

"Rabbit stick," she explained. "He turned himself into a rabbit stick."

"A rabbit stick? What's that got to do with flyin?"

"Everything. Once he twisted his body into the shape of a rabbit stick, he could ride the wind."

"I still don't understand, grand-ma. What's a rabbit stick?"

"I've only seen a few, when I was a girl. Timicuan hunters didn't use rabbit sticks because we were mountain dwellers, but the Chich-uilla tribe, who lived in the flat-lands and forests below us, used them to hunt rabbits and small game.

"You find a long piece of cedar or mesquite, hard wood, bend it into the shape of a bow, smooth it out, take a sharp piece of obsidian to cut and scrape it into just the right shape and dimensions. You carve it and sand it and polish it till it is smooth and flat and the edges can slice through the air. And when you get that shape just right, you throw the stick into the wind and it will ride on the current like a wing. A good hunter could hit a rabbit from one hundred yards away with the right current and a well-shaped stick. Each hunter had his own particular style of throwing, and each stick had its own particular way of flying depending on the design."

Well, I was somewhat confabu-lated by this

explanation.

Rabbit sticks and snakes, I didn't see the connection.

And I sure didn't see how either one could fly.

I mean a snake's a snake ain't it?

A snake ain't a bird.

A snake don't have wings and feathers and eyes that can see from far off where they're going 'fore they get there.

A snake is an earthbound creature.
They got's snake-feet and snake-hands along their bellies so they can run over the ground and spread the grass blades apart and climb trees and hang

from branches and the like.

They got's 'bout much in common with a bird as I do.

But my eyes didn't lie.

I'd seen Junior rise up with the currents, and glide a mile away from where he started, and then change direction, and swirl and twirl his way back to earth as gentle as any winged creature.

I'd seen him, and I knowed if what he done wasn't flyin', than I didn't know what flyin' was.

By this time, the crowd had carried Junior back to where me and grandma was standin', and was still chantin "Flyer! Flyer! Flyer!".

I knowed what they wanted.

They wanted to see Junior go on another flight to make sure what they seen in the first place weren't merely a figment of their imagin-ations, and to experience the adren-aline rush of Junior's death-defyin' feat.

But I weren't up for it.

Not till I could understand for myself what happened in the sky and somehow catch up to Junior's leap in creature evolution.

I could see Slim was also a little spooked by his son's sudden jump from snake-twirlin' to snake-flyin', and so when the crowd chanted to me for a repeat performance, I lied and said my arm was all played out, and I needed a day to rest.

Disappointment blew through the crowd, then someone yelled "Flyer! Flyer!" again and off they went, Junior ridin' on top of a firemen's hat like an antenna tunin' into a station only flyers could hear.

Grandma and I turned and walked quietly back to our house, each burning with our own reflectin' thoughts.

The Next Day,

as I was on my way to visit the Snake Clan, I seen Billy sittin' under a weepin' willow as I was crossing the vacant field.

I never really talked to him at school after me and Slim saved him, but he was wearing such a hangdog look and sad face, I couldn't help but sit down beside him.

"You still upset 'bout what happened?"

"Naw. It ain't that. I didn't want to be part of the Bad Boy gang anyhow so it didn't matter much when they kicked me out after the fall. I mean I was sore for awhile after they had me run through the gauntlet and paddled me for breaking the 'Never Show Fear Rule'."

"They paddled you?"

"Yeah. The Bad Boyz gauntlet. You gotta run through the line of ping pong paddling Bad Boyz. Kind of a tradition with them. Use it for all sorts of initiations and punishments, especially breaking one of their ten Bad Boyz rules."

"Well, there weren't nothin' you did deserved punishment. They was just lucky me and Slim was there to catch you."

"They said I messed everything up."

"You didn't mess nothin' up. I already knowed they was up to some kind of mischief when they invited me. So if'n it ain't that, than what's ailin' you?"

"I don't want to talk about it."

"If you don't talk about it, how you gonna get it outta you?"

"I doodle. Make pictures. That helps."

"Making pictures ain't helping you much today far as I can see."

"I just can't seem to find a picture for what I'm feeling, that's all."

"Maybe there ain't no picture for what you're feeling?"

"There's a picture for every feeling, a color too though sometimes it's hard to see it."

"Well, I don't see nothin' in that picture 'bout what's ailin' you, nor in what you said neither."

And then I was silent figurin' if the quiet got loud enough maybe he'd find the words for what was makin' his face so long. But Billy just kept gazin' into his doodle pad like I weren't even there.

The quiet kept getting' louder and louder and finally got so loud that it was all I could hear, the quiet, and my breathin', and Billy's pencil scratchin' away at the doodle pad tryin' to find a picture for what he felt.

"Well, if you ain't talkin', I ain't stayin'." I said as I got up to leave.

Billy looked up from his doodle pad and asked me a question like the sky above was cracked and ready to fall if'n he couldn't puzzle out an answer.

"You understand math?"

"Yeah. No. Some, I guess." I said.

"Fractions?"

"Yeah. Most, less they get so small I can't imagine them."

"I don't. Not a single one. How can something be half or a quarter of what it used to be?"

"A quarter's a quarter. Don't make it less than whole just cause it ain't got it's wholeness with it anymore."

"That's what I don't get. And that's why they're gonna hold me back."

"Hold you back? A grade? For not understandin' fractions?"

And then it was like a waterfall of words fallin' out his mouth.

Billy said the Principal told his parents they were going to have to hold him back a grade since his math skills were so poor. He said he used to be okay in math, but after the snake-scarin' incident, no mat-ter how hard he tried, he just couldn't understand fractions no more.

Now I Knowed

this weren't the whole problem and there was somethin' else 'neath this problem that was probably the root of the real problem.

"That's all they did, just made you run through a gauntlet and paddled you with ping pong paddles?"

"Yeah. And made me take a vow of silence."

"Don't sound right to me. You sure?"

"They made me swear in blood and said if I ever told anyone about their secret rituals and initiations they would make me swallow a snake's head. Then they killed a snake and made me kiss the head to seal the vow."

"They killed a snake and made you kiss the head?"

"Yeah. As part of the ritual. They kill snakes as part of all their rituals."

"Oh, that's bad, that's really, really bad."

And then I started worryin' 'bout Slim and the rest of his family.

I was ready to go warn him when Billy stopped me.

"Rainbo, wait. What's bad?"

"Killin' a snake and kissin' the head. That's what put the curse on you?"

"I've got a curse on me. Oh, Rainbo, what am I going to do?"

"No wonder them Bad Boyz gots such bad spirits. What'd that snake-head look like? Didn't look like Slim, did he?"

"No. He was black with red and yellow stripes."

"King snake. Coulda been a lot worse. But kissin' a severed King snake's head steals wholeness from the brain. Don't let you remember how to put pieces back together to make a whole."

"You mean like fractions."

"Yeah, fractions, parts, segments like the way a snake's body's made. Cut the head from the body and the body never be able to find the head that it belongs to. You was lucky though. If'n woulda been Slim or one of his relatives, I couldn't have helped you."

"You can help me?"

"Maybe. I think you need an anti-curse."

"A what?"

59

"An anti-curse. A curse that cancels out the original curse like an anecdote for rat poison."

"How do you know all this about curses and stuff? Are you really a witch?"

"No. That's just a rumor your brother and the Bad Boys started to save face after their snake-scarin' fiasco. My grandmother's a curan-dera, a healer, but that ain't the same. She knows white magic. She don't cast no evil spells on a body. What magic I gots I gots from her."

"She...uh...can help me?"

"She don't...I mean...she stopped healin' people a while ago 'causa her forgetfulness disease. But she might have

60

somethin' in her potion book to heal you."

"Can we go ask her?

"Look Billy, if'n I can help you I will, but I ain't guaranteein' nothin'. You shoulda known better than take part in somethin' that causes an innocent bein' to be hurt or killed. You gots to own part of the responsibility, which is why the curse is causin' you such confusion. Besides, my grandma ain't been herself lately..."

Billy started doodlin' on his doodle-pad somethin' fierce.

At first I just thought it was on account of him bein' so upset and all, but when I looked over and seen what he was doodlin' I realized it was a lot more than that.

See Billy didn't really live in *this* world, at least not the way you and I live in it.

I mean he ate peanut butter and jelly sandwiches and liked sour apple candies and Snickers and Bubblegum Ice Cream same as you and me, but if'n you asked Billy a question, (before the curse anyway), like who's George Washington, or what's the capital of New York, he probably give you an answer that woulda made you think he was from Mars or Jupiter or somewhere. I heard a teacher once asked Billy to name the President of the United States and Billy started namin' off the ten reindeer pullin' Santa Claus' sled includin' red-nosed Rudolph. No one realized of course it was Christmas time and Billy was doodlin' Christmas greetings on his doodle-pad. And what he was tryin' to remember at that very same moment, was what was the names of all them reindeer was, so he could write them under their pictures.

Now I knowed some kids be doodlin' simply 'cause they be bored. They be sittin' in the back of the room all scrunched down and hidin' and be drawin' some squiggles that don't mean nothin' 'cept in their own private conversations with themselves.

And maybe those squiggles look like some creatures from prehistoric times or from a cartoon they seen on television.

But Billy's doodles told a story and owned a meanin' and a lan-guage of their own.

I s'ppose people didn't listen to Billy 'cause he was so shy and quiet all the time.

But all they had to do was give him a little attention, listen for more'n two minutes straight, and they woulda seen he weren't from outer space, but right here beside them, and offered a whole lot more'n most people had to say.

And the thing was, once Billy got over his shyness with a person, why he'd open up like one of those Angel Trumpets grandma showed me, all fragrant and beatific like they was planted by the Great Spirit herself.

'Cause that's what Billy was, a spirit-gift, even though nobody took the time to see it.

They seen him the same way they seen me most of the time: Someone who don't fit into their idea of what a body should be.

"Rainbow! Rainbow B. Seed, didn't your mother teach you to respect your Elders?" Miss Prince would say to me when I give her back some sass to go with her pompousness.

"No, my mama's too busy workin' three jobs to teach me much 'bout respect. But my grandma, she say you gotta give respect to receive respect, and some people don't know how to respect nothin' but their own misconceptions of the world."

Well, that got her blood boilin' alright.

I didn't care.

I think I was born dislikin' the Miss Prince's of the world, and maybe that's why the Great Spirit put me here in the first place.

Anyways, I knowed all 'bout that alien being stuff so I didn't pay it no mind.

But I also knowed a gift when I seen one, and when I looked at Billy's doodlin' that's exactly what I seen.

See, Billy's doodle-picture put me and him and the snakehead and the curse and the Bad Boyz all in perspective.

There were balloons comin' out of everybody's mouth like they knew what they was talkin' 'bout.

And they all wore expressions like they knew more'n they was sayin'.

And their doodle-faces was funny, like an ironic caricature.

They looked like who they was was, but they was exaggerated in such a way to tell a truth 'bout who they really were.

Some, like Max, had big heads and small bodies, and some, like the King snake, had small heads and big bodies.

Some looked radiant as angels, and some were ugly as Tasmanian Devils.

There was fractions floatin' through the sky like musical notes, and at the bottom was the caption, "A curse of fractions rules the world."

"Can I look through your doodle-book, Billy?"

"I guess, long as you don't make fun of me."

"I wouldn't do that. I just want to see what else you doodled."

"Okay, but you promise, right?"

"I promise."

He handed me the book and I started flippin' through page after page mesmerized by the picture-stories he told.

There was Miss Prince and her teacher's pets waddlin'

across a lake, 'cept they all had human heads on duck bodies.

At the bottom of the page was a caption "A School For Ducks". Another page showed Max and the Bad Boyz up in a tree holdin' ping pong paddles, 'cept they didn't have human heads, they had parrot heads, and they was all squawkin' "Kill! Kill! Kill!" from a balloon comin' out of their mouth, and a caption read, "Want to play Parrot Pong?"

"You got's to put these stories in a book," I tells him after awhile.

"I'm no book writer. I'm a doodler."

"You're a book writer same as anyone who tells stories, 'sides what you gonna do when you grow up, go down to one of them hamburger stands and wrap up people's Fat-burgers for 'em. You got's the gift of drawin' stories, Billy, and makin' people laugh when they see them. Ain't no gift puttin' people's beef patties between two buns that taste like stale cardboard and tellin' 'em to have a nice day when you know the nicest their day's gonna be is when they go home and sit in front of the television and watch some one else's misery so they don't have to think 'bout their own.

"I'm never gonna work in one of those places. I hate hamburgers. I hate even thinking about the cows they killed to put between those buns."

"Well, that's why you got's to use your gift, Billy. People needs to hear stories that tell the truth and make them laugh."

"You think my stories are funny?"

"Funny, in a serious kind of way. Funny, to make people see what's right in front of their noses. Funny, the way grandma is funny with her odd ways and her wisdom-riddles. Funny, with a bitter-sweet taste of truth."

"I thought you liked them?"

"I do like them. I like them 'specially 'cause they're true in the way only a picture or a story can be true. I like them 'cause your doodle-pictures make you different from every body else."

"My brother says my stories are weird. He says they make no sense. And Miss Prince told my mother last year I oughtta see the school psychiatrist 'bout my doodling. Last time a teacher seen my doodles I got sent to the Principal's office and my mama got called in to figure out what was wrong with me. That's why I don't let people see what I'm doodling anymore."

"Ain't nothin' wrong with you 'cept what people be jealous of, Billy. Your brother Max is 'bout as brainless as one of them video game heroes. He's got nothing better to do but torment and bully people to make himself feel special. Him and the Bad Boyz go up in that tree house of theirs and plan wars on people like they was their own separate army. 'Cept there ain't no war goin' on, just the war inside their own fool heads. And you know what's gonna happen? When they grow up, they's gonna find somebody else's war, and stick that inside their heads too, and then they gonna play war for real, and they gonna find out it ain't as excitin' and painless as them video games.

I knowed that 'cause my grandma told me how her whole tribe got killed in a war, and there weren't no people left to pass on their stories 'cept the children.

And Miss Prince done had her head shrunk so many times there ain't nothin' good left between her shrunken ears 'cept what she wants to hear to make her own self feel good. Miss Prince got 'bout as much sense as a walnut, which is probably 'bout the size of her brain now that it's been shrunk so many times.

Your doodles tell stories 'bout real people, 'bout kids like you and me dealin' with the things we deal with at school and at home and whereever we go. That's a gift, and you needs to give that gift back to people no matter what fools like Miss Prince and your brother and anybody else be sayin."

"You really think I've been given a gift?"

"Does a zebra have spots? I mean look at this picture," and I opened the page to a bright-colored doodle of a boy. "This boy's lookin' for his lost lucky rabbit's foot, right?"

"A feather. He's looking for a red feather...from a hawk."

"So he's looking for his lucky red feather?"

"Yeah."

"And then this teacher comes, Miss Prince probably, 'cept she's got horns, which Miss Prince probably has, but we just can't see them."

"How'd you know it was Miss Prince? I thought I'd disguised her by making her tall and spidery with five arms."

"What other teacher look like that with horns on?"

"I put a beard on her, but then she started looking like a preying mantis so I erased it."

"A beard woulda been too much. Anyway, she starts sayin' bad words to the boy, and he sees the feather fluttering down from a cloud, and then he plucks it, and waves it in front of her, and suddenly she turns into a horny toad. Now, if'n that ain't the best, most funniest story 'bout mean teachers, I don't know what is. Why it's downright inspirin'."

"You like it that much?"

" 'Course I like it, and a lotta other people would like it too if they seen it.

75

That feather is the kind of magic most people wish for 'cause most people just get bullied by the Max'es and the Miss Prince's of the world.

Most people wishes they had a red feather to wave at all them people with horns."

Billy looked at me, and we held eyes for a long time, and it was like when Slim and me first whispered, and I knew from that moment on, me and Billy was gonna be best friends.

Still, I Didn't Know

if grandma could help him.

Spells and curses weren't in grandma's purview.

She was a curandera, not a witch.

And if it weren't in her potion book, I didn't see her creating a new one 'causa her forgetfulness disease.

But, I couldn't just not help Billy, snake-killin' or not.

So, Billy walked home with me, and we asked her.

"Grandma, do you have an anti-curse potion?"

"A what?"

"A potion that kills a curse."

"What kind of a curse?"

"Billy killed a snake on account of the Bad Boyz Club, and now he can't understand fractions."

"Killing a snake won't cause a curse to be put on you. It won't give you good luck or a life of harmony with the Great Spirit, but a curse, now that's a horse of a different being."

"But what the Bad Boyz done was more'n just killin' a snake, grandma. They cut off the head and took an oath on it."

"They cut off a head!? And kissed it!? And took an oath on it!? That's bad. That's really bad. That's black magic, and that's going to cause you all sorts of spirit problems, and that will require an extremely strong anti-potion and an anti-oath ritual besides.

Let me see..." and she started thumbin' through her potion book."

"Yes, right here......anti-curse ...anti-ritual...anti-spell...anti-...anti-...hmmm...I don't have an 'anti-oath' potion, Rainbo."

"Can't you just use an anti-curse potion?"

"Well, maybe. But a curse is a curse and an oath is an oath, and you never know what you're going to get. If you use the wrong potion, you might get the wrong cure. I once gave a woman an anti-love potion so she would fall out of love with a dreadful young man. Except, I didn't have the necessary red rose petals so I thought I could replace them with some pink rose petals. But pink rose petals are for good health and long life and not love or anti-love. Turned out, it was the worse thing I could've done, and ended up being the worse potion I ever made."

"What happened?"

"After she drank that potion, she turned into a fat toad."

"What?! Snakes alive, grandma, I thought you couldn't turn people into toads!?"

"Oh, Rainbo, sometimes you are so naïve!" and she laughed her cackle laugh. "I was just exagger-ating to make a point!

My potions can't turn people into toads. But the pink petals had the opposite effect of what I intended. Not only did she not fall out of love with the young man, she fell more in love with him, and married him, and gave birth to nine dreadful children. Her children turned out to be the worst liars, thieves, and despicable people the State of Florida ever knew. The worst one even became President of the United States for a time, 'till they kicked him out of office. He even went to jail on account of all his lying."

Billy, who was sitting all quiet and respectful, finally burst out in tears.

"Ma-am, I'm sorry, I'm...I'm...so sorry for kissing that snake's head and saying bad things, but I'm going to fail, and then I'm going to have to

82

quit school and take a job a Burger Queen flipping hamburgers for the rest of my life. Please ma-am, can't you give any potion to fix me? I think I'd rather be a fat toad than a hamburger flipper. I hate hamburgers. And if I can't ever understand fractions, how am I ever gonna understand wholes, or be a whole person again."

"Calm down, son. Let's see what I can do. Okay. Snakes are seg-mented. That's how they can grow their tails back and such. Seems like you have a segmentation problem. On account of you going against the natural laws of nature by severing the snake's head and then kissing it? What oath did you say?"

"Wasn't really an oath. Was more like a spell. 'Kill a snake.

Kiss a snake. Be a snake too.' We said it three times, then we kissed and buried the snakehead."

"Oh, that's bad. That's a black witch's spell. That's going to take one of my strongest potions to change it. Let's see......war... warts... weapons... here we go......whole ......wholes......wholeness...wholesome...

...maybe if I gave you a potion that made you wholesome again? Might work.

Now let's see if we have all the ingredients we need."

Grandma opened up her medi-cine pouch and laid out various leaves and herbs and essences.

There was dried sassafras berries, and locks of jack rabbit fur, and flakes of horny toad skin.

And there was powder of ground up rattlesnake fangs, and dust of rosemary and thyme, and bits and buds of flowers and plants and claws and teeth and skin from creatures I never knew.

I was surprised at how she seemed to suddenly remember every element of her "Notion & Potion Book", and what ingredient was missing from a particular potion.

"No, that's not right," she kept saying as she looked at her various potions.

"This one needs a pluck of jasmine flower." And she would write in the missing ingredient.

85

"And this one doesn't have dust from a wolf's claw."

She must have gone through ten or twelve potions before she got back to the wholesome one.

Then she mixed together a cup of five or six ingredients, poured in a little spring water from the Alachua mountains, and handed it to Billy.

"Drink this, and let me know how you feel."

Billy looked at grandma with the same fear as when he first saw Slim, then suddenly grabbed the cup and drank the potion down in one gulp.

His face turned green and then blue and then red and I

thought he was gonna throw up, but instead he starts spouting:

"The sum of the square roots of any two sides of an isosceles triangle is equal to the square root of the remaining side. And the sum of one fifty-ninth added to one hundred and five fifty-ninths is equal to the sum of—"

"Billy?! Billy?! Grandma!!!"

"Let him be, Rainbo. He's in a wholesome trance right now. He'll come out of it as soon as the potion circulates through his entire body."

Billy babbled on for a while, then his face turned back to normal and he looked at us with bright clear eyes.

"Wow! Uh...uh...I feel...I feel... really smart!!! Ask me a fraction, Rainbo?"

"How much is one-half and one-half?"

"One. Ask me something harder."

"How much is one quarter and three quarters?"

"One. Something harder."

"How much is nine fifths and three fifths?"

"Twelve fifths, or two and two fifths. Oh, thank you, Miss Wolf. Thank you. I can do fractions again. I'm cured! I'm cured. Oh, thank you. Thank you."

Grandma starred at Billy for a moment, then drank the remainder of the wholesome potion.

Her face turned green, blue, and red, then back to normal, 'cept now it owned a radiant glow.

"I don't know why I never thought of this. Wholeness. That's what my memory was missing. Whole memories. Whole visions. Being whole. Billy, I think your fraction potion is going to cure us both!"

Grandma's forgetfulness got better after that, but I was never sure if it was Billy's potion, or if it had to do with becoming a snake-woman.

I Was Still Perplexed

'bout Junior's snake-flyin' and I weren't 'bout to repeat the exper-ience till I could hold it between my ears.

I asked Billy if'n he ever heard of such a thing as a rabbit stick, or if'n he knew a theory that could explain Junior's flyin'.

"Aerodynamics." Billy replied.
"Air-o-who?"
"Aerodynamics, the principles of flying. It's how birds glide on the currents and how planes stay up in the air and how when you throw a boomerang away it turns around and comes back to your hand."
"You're tellin' me Junior learned how to do air-o-dy-nam-ics and that's how he learned to fly?"
"He probably just figured out how to make his body imitate a

bird's wing and got lucky. Could've backfired."

"Backfired? What do you mean?"

"I mean aerodynamics doesn't always mean you're gonna catch the currents right and rise up like a feather catching a breeze. If he'd caught the currents at the wrong angle, or flattened his body out in a way that ran counter to the wind, or turned it slightly in the wrong direction, well..."

"Well what?"

"Well the current might've pushed him straight down toward the ground instead of up toward the clouds."

"Ground would've caught up to him before I could've reached him."

"Yeah, most likely. Flying looks a lot easier than it is. The Wright Brothers crashed over a hundred planes before they ever got one to fly."

"Junior didn't seem too worried 'bout crashin'."

"Maybe Junior's a daredevil and likes danger."

"Well, I ain't takin' no chances again. I'm gonna talk to Slim 'bout groundin' him."

"People are probably going to expect to see him fly, Rainbo, and sooner or later, he's probably going to try to fly again."

"Well, I ain't gonna be the one tossin' him up into the sky again, so he ain't gonna fly."

"People have been trying to fly ever since they saw the first bird glide on the wind and wished they could do the same."

"Junior ain't a person."

"I think even snakes wish they were birds some times."

"Wishin' don't make it so."

"Your snake-twirling inspires people, Rainbo, shows them how anything is possible. Most people never imagined someone could do such a thing."

Billy was right.

Still, twirlin' and flyin' were two different things and I weren't sure I wanted any part of the flyin' cause of the danger and all.

So that afternoon I decided to have a pow-wow with Slim.

"I need to talk to you 'bout Junior."
"Junior's grounded." Slim whis-pered.
Last night after his flight, the Elders met. Although we were all amazed by Junior's prowess, the Elders believe flying is against

snake-nature. They made a decree: 'No snake-flying.' If any snake tries to fly again they will be banished from the clan."

"Slim, Junior isn't the only snake who wants to fly. I heard some of the younger snakes whisperin' they wished they'd been the first."

"Snakes are snakes. Snakes aren't birds. Snakes are earthbound crea-tures and birds are skybound creatures. The Elders believe if we start trying to be something we're not we are going to bring a bad omen upon ourselves."

"What 'bout the twirlin'?"

"Twirling is different. The Elders believe twirling is a good thing because it was prophesied in the Great Oracle. The Oracle tells of a human who leads the snake clan out of the darkness of the old world with a new vision, and leads us into the light of the future. The Elders believe you were the one prophesied by the oracle. They believe you twirling me up into the sky was foretold many, many gen-erations ago. But what Junior did yesterday wasn't foretold in the prophesy. If we let our youth be free to imitate sky-creatures who knows where it will end. We'll have our young leaping out of trees because they believe they were meant to fly. Snakes will start falling out of the sky and crash to the ground. Many will be injured or die. No, Rainbo. The Oracle is clear: No flying. Junior is grounded until he can abide by that rule."

Once Slim and I had our pow-wow, he whispered into the

knothole and the rest of the clan crawled out and gathered round in a circle.

They were twirlin' snakes now, and ever would be.

They would whirl and swirl and twirl till each saw the sky as a brother to the earth, but they would not fly because flyin' was the domain of sky-creatures and not the domain of snakes.

Well, it may have been decreed by the Elders, but not all the snakes agreed.

Some thought Junior's punishment was too harsh.

Some thought the Oracle was wrong.

Some didn't see much

difference between twirlin' and flyin'.

I knew today's snake-twirlin show wasn't gonna be like any in the past.

Whoever went first would have to cross an imaginary line between those for snake-twirlin' and those for snake-flyin', a line between young and old, between the future and the past, between what was and what could be.

And me, I stood smack-dab in the middle.

I believed in the Elders and I believed in Junior's leap of genius.

I believed in the Oracle and I believed in the possible world beyond.

I believed in history and the history a flyin' prodigy like Junior could make anew.

So I stood on that line and waited for someone to be the first.

No one moved. The no-flyin' decree and bein' the first to cross that imaginary line froze every snake in their place.

There would be no snake-twirlin' today, maybe never again.

The crowd got restless.

A low chant of "Flyer! Flyer! Flyer!" began to reverberate through the throng, then "Junior, Junior, Junior".

But Junior was nowhere to be found.

After the Elders grounded him and announced the "no-flyin' rule" Junior angrily crawled away and no one had seen him since.

"The Elders are just too old and afraid to accept a new vision of the Snake Clan," he shouted as he left.

"He's a little stubborn," said Slim, "but over time, he'll learn it was for his own good. We all want to change the world when we're young."

I wasn't so sure Junior would give up flyin'. He was a genius of the air. Bein' grounded went against his nature.

Finally Slim realized no one was gonna break the impasse. If there was gonna be a show, if the snakes were ever gonna be twirlers again, he, Slim, would have to lead the way.

So Slim slowly crawled up my arm and into my palm and looked round at the crowd.

"All right, Rainbo, three swirls and a full twist," Slim whispered.
"Are you sure?"
"Sure."

I grasped Slim midway between his head and his tail and heaved him up as high as I could.
I saw him begin his first swirl as he passed above the crown of the oak. His second swirl and twist started as he slowly descended down.

Then out of the corner of my eye, I saw somethin' dive out of the oak's topmost branches.

I thought maybe it was a squirrel, or a bird hoppin' from one tree to the next, but it didn't look like no squirrel, or no bird neither. Looked more like a bent twig, or a broken branch. And it was fallin' fast, fallin' like any other branch fallin' except in mid-air it moved slightly, bent a little, and I knowed it was no twig, not even a rabbit stick. It was Junior, Junior divin' out of the crown of that tree, Junior tryin' to fly!

Well, you can imagine the fear that jumped into my throat when I realized it was Junior fallin', while his father, Slim, was just a few feet ahead of him in his own fall.

Now maybe I could've been

quick enough to catch one and then the other in each of my hands. Or maybe I could've laid down on my back and let each one bounce off my belly when they fell.

But there was a problem.

Each was fallin' on opposite sides of the tree.

There was no way I was gonna be quick 'enuff to run from one side of the tree to the other and catch both.

One.
One or the other.
Father or son.
Slim, or Junior.
One was gonna be caught, and one was gonna smash into the ground.

Guess 'bout the same time as I came to this conclusion, so did half the crowd.

Someone screamed.
Someone moaned.
Some put their hands over their eyes.

"Billy!" I shrieked.

But Billy was already under the spot where Slim was comin' down with his palms open wide, waitin'.

I ran to the other side of the oak just as Junior was streakin' past the last branches.

Slim landed with a loud plop in Billy's palms, and I waited for Junior.

Just a half-second more,

then…

Nothing!

One moment Junior was droppin' like a stone, and the next, he was gone.

Quicker than our eyes could see, quicker than I could run to catch him, Junior caught a strong current and rose up above the crown of the oak, whirlin' 'round like the whirlin' rotor of a helicopter.

No use tryin' to follow him now.

He'd risen over the crown and gone out over the deep woods, a blurry speck flyin' over the tops of trees.

By now, Billy had gotten over

bein' face to face with another
snake.

He was a little scared, but he
was okay, and Slim was still
dazed from the fall.

When Slim came to his senses
and realized Billy was holdin'
him, he smiled and slithered out
of Billy's palms and down to the
ground.

But no one was payin'
attention to Billy and Slim.

Their eyes was focused on
where that black speck of
Junior'd disappeared in the sky.

And then, suddenly, out of
the blue, streakin' toward us
from the opposite direction from
where he disappeared, came
Junior, a black speck growin'
larger in the middle of the sun.

And then, Junior whirled past,

a few feet above our heads, and we was all mesmerized, caught up in Junior's spectacular aerial display.

He spun past us so fast we had to jerk our heads round to follow him, then he seemed to catch another wave and began a long, slow circle 'round the oak and up into the sky.

Up, up into the clouds and gone again.

And there weren't no doubtin' now.

He weren't a snake no more.

He weren't Junior, son of Slim, offspring of the Snake Clan.

He was somethin' else, some

new creation.

He was "Wing", "Flyer", "Snake-Hawk", or "Sky-Creature".

He was the vision the Elders never saw.

He was the earthbound future, a divin' and glidin' presence circlin' in a slow arc 'round the oak and through the clouds above.

'Least that's the way he seemed to me as he banked 'round and came whirlin' down a few feet above our heads again.

'Cept this time I could see somethin' weren't right.

He was havin' a hard time keeping his body bowed and flat against the strong currents.

He was wobblin' and flappin'

and bouncin' up and down like he was negotiatin' bumps in the road.

He was hittin' turbulence and buckin' this way and that ridin' on a buckin' bronco of wind.

So, when he circled 'round a second time, he was bobbin' and bouncin' and buckin' too low.

He dipped down and ricocheted off of someone's head and then off of someone else's shoulder.

He caught his balance again, but was flyin' so low he plowed into a ladies summer hat and spun 'round like he had a flyin' saucer over his body.

Then he skidded off the ground like he was a smooth stone bouncin' off the surface of a green lake. 'Cept it wasn't water he was bouncin' off of, it was the hard ground, and that ground was strewn with large rocks growin' out of the weeds, and if Junior dipped down and hit one of them, he was gonna be squished, and we was all gonna walk away sad.

By now, people were jumpin' this way and that tryin to get out of Junior's way.

He would dip down and hit the earth, or some one's body, and then he would bounce up two or three feet in the air, and then dive down again, the bow of his body changin' into a crooked stick and then bendin' back to a bow.

He turned 'round the oak and flew back 'round again circlin' the crowd no higher then six inches off the ground.

Well, I don't know if it was

my snake-twirlin' instinct or what, but when he come 'round a second time I leaped out in front of him and caught him in my hand.

The force of catchin' him spinnin' in full flight threw me into the air and spun us both 'round five or six times 'till we both tumbled down.

I rolled over and over and over cradlin' Junior 'gainst my body 'till I finally stopped rollin'.

I was layin' on my back, and Junior was wrapped tight 'gainst my belly, and the crowd was screamin' and cheerin' like I'd just scored a goal, or hit a grand slam homerun, or some other sports highlight.

But Junior weren't movin'.

He lay against my belly limp

as a worm, and I didn't know if'n he was in shock, or if'n he was unconscious, or if'n he was dead.

Snakes came out from everywhere.

Out of knotholes, and caves, and gopher holes, and the nooks of branches and the crevices of rocks.

Slim and the rest of the Snake Clan crawled to Junior and slithered over and 'round and under Junior's body to rouse him.

His little brothers slid under Junior's head and licked his face to wake him.

His little sisters snuggled against Junior's tail.

Still, Junior didn't move.

If he was alive, he weren't tellin'.

112

I couldn't feel no heartbeat, and his body was cool as the moist earth 'gainst my back.

A gray cloud drifted over the oak an' cast a dark shadow across the field.

Little by little, the crowd wan-dered away.

After awhile, there was no one left but Slim, and the snake family, and me, and Billy, and grandma.

Some of the snake family was whisperin' to Junior, but some was cryin' too, 'cause I could hear the weepin' through the whispers, and the heavy sighs of grief through the sad breaths.

Grandma sat down beside me, and took Junior in her palms.

Then she started a soft, low chant that sounded like a wish, or a thanks, or a question, and I didn't know if'n she was singin' to heal Junior, or to wake him, or if it were a song to keep him company on his journey to the other world.

And I don't think Billy, or the snake clan knowed either.

But we all joined in anyway, and sang those low notes softly, in harmony, like a chorus of believers, 'cause it didn't matter whether 'twas a song to raise spirits and bring Junior back from the spirit world, or 'twas a song for the ones left behind to sing goodbye as Junior passed on.

We sang, and grandma chanted, and the gray dusk turned to violet and to purple and to black, and then the darkness became a hand and held us as we sang softly through the night.

Now I Ain't Gonna Say

there was ever a miracle more wondrous than the one we witnessed when the sun broke over the horizon and a dim pink light rose from the oaks.

Nor that there was a wonder more miraculous than Billy, and grandma, and me, and Slim, and the snakes, and squirrels, and birds, and all the rest of the creatures mournin' Jun-ior's passin' with our sad, reverent song.

Nor that there was ever a song or a prayer more wondrous, nor a gesture more lovin' than grandma preparin' a buryin' salve of sage and crushed rattlesnake rattles and yuc-ca flowers, and wrappin' Junior up with dried fig leaves, and layin' him down at the foot of that tree.

I wouldn't say that 'cause it wouldn't be true.

'Cause the truth is there never was such a song, nor a gesture, nor a prayer more wondrous than ours, and maybe that's why when the bright morning light come, Junior slowly fluttered open his eyes, and whis-pered to Slim, and finally came back to this world.

Now I know Junior's wakin' weren't as spectacular as them stories 'bout Jesus walkin' on water or Moses partin' the Red Sea.

I mean weren't like the earth stood still, or the moon turned blue, or a green shootin' star shot across the sky. (Grandma says a new constellation was formed in the night sky that night, the constellation of "The Flying Snake", but I never could see them pictures made out of stars so I can't say one way or the other.)

But it was a true miracle all the same.

And things changed, even if they weren't so visible as volcanoes eruptin' and such.

Junior sure weren't the same.

When he first come back from his deep sleep, he just lay all bruised and achin' in grandma's bed of palms and barely stirred.
But as the days passed little by little, he got stronger and stronger and started to crawl again and there was somethin' different 'bout him.
He seemed to glow with a

strange radiance like his skin collected and reflected sun.

When he slid over the grass, he was iridescent with all the colors of the rainbow and emanated golden light.

When he whispered, his words rolled off his tongue slow and easy and sounded like they come from some deep place beyond his body.

And he never said much, maybe only two or three words at a time, but each word seemed to rise up out of the ground beneath him like a grass blade or sagebrush sprout.

No, he weren't snake no more.

He was a new creature crawlin' out of grandma's cocoon of fig leaves learnin' to be new.

And grandma changed.

She didn't live in our house no more.

She slept out under the oak tree with Junior and all the Snake Clan curled up 'round her.

She became a snake-woman curandera and mixed powerful new potions from the petals of blue flowers she collected from deep in the forest.

And she got her memory back.

She could remember as far back now as when she was a baby ridin' in a papoose on her mother's back.

She could remember the sweet smell of sassafras and licorice root and the feel of the horsehair blanket against her skin.

She could remember each day like it was the first day she'd arrived on this earth, and it didn't matter whether that day was fifty years ago, or yesterday past.

And Billy changed.

After catchin' Slim and savin' his life, Billy weren't afraid of snakes no more.
He learned to snake-whisper, and wear snakes round his neck and arms, and even twirl a few up into the sky.

And when he weren't whisperin', or twirlin', he was drawin' snakes, and even started creatin' a book of snakes which he called "Rainbow In Paradise". (Now I never understood that title, but Billy said he wanted to recreate one of them creation myths he read about, and that me and the Snake Clan was the bestest remakin' of creation he could ima-gine.)

And the snake clan changed too.

The "No Flying" rule changed to "Live To Fly", which the Elders said meant that "all snakes wished to fly" even if snakes weren't born with wings.

The Oracle was reinterpreted to foretell the present: Junior's flight foretold the future.

A "School For Twirlers And Flyers" would be formed for Junior and I to teach the present and fu-ture generations of snakes. Flyin' as well as twirlin' would be part of our shows.

Even I changed some.

I learned it weren't so much how you looked, or how old you were, or what your physical limitations were, but who and what you *believed* you were that mattered.

If you believed you *could fly*, and if you practiced and practiced and tried hard enough, well, it didn't matter whether you was a snake, or a squirrel, or a human, you would some day learn to fly.

'Course none of this happened over night mind you.

Junior had to heal, and the flyin' school had to be created, and none of us really knowed what we was doin' till we'd done it.

Summer slipped into Fall.

Leaves turned into all the colors of the earth, and then dropped from the trees to join the cycle of seasons.

Me and Billy went back to school and only saw the Snake Clan on Saturdays and Sundays.

We performed a few shows on the weekends to keep in shape, but Junior was still healin' and the "Flyin' School" was still a Spring away.

Fall drifted into Winter, and the vacant field grew a beard of snow, and the Snake Clan brumated in knotholes and crevices and coiled up close together for warmth during their long slumber.

By the time Spring came

again, grandma was a full "snake-woman curandera".

Each night she dreamt of snakes whisperin' to her from the other world.

She said they gave her messages for the future, and secret potions to heal all the hurt creatures of the world.

Her arthritis went away, and her joints stopped swellin' up and achin', and she started makin' turquoise rings and bracelets like she did when she was young.

She made turquoise rings for the entire snake clan, and slipped them over their heads, and called them "Snakes of Turquoise Stone".

The rings actually turned out to be a perfect tool for trainin' the snakes to fly.

126

See, snakes have great muscle control for crawling over the ground.

They can slide their head, or their belly, or their tail over rocks, and leaves, and logs, and up the trunks and branches of trees, but if you asked them to bend or turn a certain muscle in a specific place on their body, well, they just couldn't connect the thought with that particular spot.

But if you touched that particular spot with your fingertip, or pressed the heat of your finger against the slippery skin on the underside of their belly, why they could twist and turn the muscle of that particular segment into a knot, or flatten it out like a flapjack.

Without that touch however, they couldn't imagine the place on their body where you wanted them to bend or twist.

No matter how many times me or Junior whispered the place, they just couldn't make the connection from their body to their mind.

They'd bend their tails into a "C", but the spot you wanted them to bend, or flatten, wouldn't even quiver.

However, if I slipped a ring down to a particular segment of their bodies though, they could feel the ring pressed against their skin and isolate that place to make it bend.

Junior didn't have this problem.

He was born with specific muscle control, or somehow he'd trained himself to have it.

Junior said he didn't have it

till he started studyin' the birds, but the Elders believed he'd possessed it all along, and that's what made him different. They said he was born with a special gift and that's what the Oracle hadn't foretold.

But, as we trained more and more of the snakes, we discovered that it weren't just Junior who had this special gift.

Many of the younger snakes possessed it as well, and even some of the older snakes could find the place in their mind that connected to specific muscles in their bodies.

Still, some snakes just couldn't bend their mid-sections into a bow no how.

Some tried bendin' into an arc and ended up lookin' like

pretzels.

Some could bend in the middle, but the muscles in their tales and necks sympathized with the bendin' and bent along with them so that they looked more like question marks or squiggles then rabbit sticks or bows.

Some couldn't bend at all 'less they was crawlin' at the time which weren't gonna help when they was flyin' through the air.

Some would leap out of trees to twirl or fly.

And some wouldn't jump out of a tree even if you lit that tree on fire.

After three weeks of try-outs

and tribulations, we ended up with our flyin' corps.

Most were younger than Junior, but there was a few from every generation.

There was even two from the Elders, a grandmother and a grand-father who'd seen so many gener-ations of snakes they could tell you stories 'bout the first snake that ever lived in the oak, and where he came from, and how many children he created.

Some were mamas and papas that were so bored with their snake life that they woulda donned wings and jumped from the crown of that oak if it meant bringin' a little excite-ment to their lives.

No, the "Flyin' Snakes" weren't nothing like we imagined.

They was different shapes and sizes and ages and colors, and some was male, and some was female, and there weren't nothin' alike about them 'cept they all came from the same original snake way back before that King James book was written sayin' the first snake was a devil and all.

They was as different as multi-farious pebbles at the bottom of a pond.

But they all had one thing in common: The gift of their bodies hearing the whisper of their minds.

Not that the rest of the clan

didn't have their moment in the sky.

There were the twirlers, and there were the flyers, and neither me, nor Slim, nor Junior, created a disparity between the two.

None of the snakes did either.

A good twirler owned just much value as a good flyer.

"Flyers" didn't look down on the "twirlers" from above, or think they was better snakes like the Miss Prince's and the Miss Williams'es of the world.

"Flyers" were the snake future, and the "twirlers" were happy to be part of that future even if they just twirled.

I guess that was the lesson

grandma needed to learn, 'cause once she seen how the flyers loved the twirlers, and vice versa, she started dreamin' me in her dreams, and saw the buffalo in the Natural History Museum gallopin' across the plains in her vision-dreams.

By the time Spring blossomed into Summer, and the field was full of wildflowers and alfalfa and three-leaved clover, "The Flyin' Snakes" was seasoned pilots and the twirlers could do combinations of twists and turns I'd only imagined a summer before.

Junior, who was now the Captain of the "flyers", was still fearless as ever.
But there was a seriousness 'bout him too, and he always made sure every flyer was

equipped with safety precautions before he allowed them to take solo flights on the wind.

He asked grandma to make tiny parachutes to attach to the rings in case cross-currents, or wind sheer, or some such natural occurrence might catch them and throw them into an irreversible spiral down.

I never imagined a parachute small enuff for snakes, but grandma said they had thousands over at the Army surplus store 'cause the Army used them to drift flares down and light the battlefield in case the enemy was tryin' to crawl toward them in the dark.

That seemed ironic to me, 'bout the Army usin' them to see humans low-crawlin' across the battleground like snakes, and us usin' the same parachutes to teach snakes to fly.

I mean, maybe if humans spent more time tryin' to learn how to fly, they wouldn't need to crawl along the ground like snakes.

That's just my opinion mind you, but it did seem like the Great Spirit had a hand in it somehow.

I guess that's how she keeps the cosmos in balance, by allowin' one thing to be exchanged for another, and by ever mixin' things up so that each creature stays in balance with the others.

I don't know.
I'm still learnin' 'bout the Great Spirit.

And, like I told you in the beginning, the world's a mystery to me, and I'm ever surprised by it's permutations.

But sometimes, when I watched "The Flyin' Snakes" bend their bodies into a wing and soar up into the turquoise sky, I wished I too could bend and flatten and rise out of the crowns of trees...

And live my life to fly.

When Your Power Animal Speaks To You

Mama never liked snakes.

She never forgot 'bout her encounter with Slim and Shadows.

According to her "good book", snakes were "the devil incarnate", and needed to be chased back into the underworld with broom-heads and shoe-soles and such.

And she believed I'd outgrown my toddler snake-infatuation after she told me about Satan, and the story of Eve, and how a snake ruined human civilization for eternity.

'Course I wasn't gonna tell her different. (Like I told you

139

already, you don't be arguing with mama about such things 'less you want to see her come at you like a Medusa head.)

So I kept "Rainbo's Snake Twirl-in' and Flyin' Show" a secret.

But, by now, people came from all over to see us.

So many people came to watch us, we could barely fit them all in our vacant field.

And, with the buzz of our show circulating the neighborhood, and grandma changing into a snake-woman curandera and getting her memory back, mama got suspicious 'bout what was goin' on.

"Where you and grandma be going after school and on weekends, Rainbo?"

"Oh, I just be practicing, mama."

"Practicing what?"

"Throwin' and catchin'."

"With grandma?"

"With Billy."

"And grandma watches?"

"Uh...yeah."

"Well, I don't understand how watching you and Billy throwing and catching balls helps give your grandma back her memory, but I ain't gonna complain 'bout good fortune."

Now I knowed I stretched the truth a bit, and maybe even told mama a white lie, but how was I gonna tell her the truth when the truth was so incredible.

Anyways, one afternoon mama

come trompin' 'cross the field where we done our practicing to see what all the commotion was 'bout.

She'd heard stories from folk in the neighborhood 'bout "Rainbo's Snake Twirlin' And Flyin' Show".

Some peoples told her "it was the best performance in town"-- 'specially since it didn't cost nothing but the seat o' your pants and your two hands clappin'.

But mama didn't believe nothing 'less she seen it with her own two eyes,--and a snake-flying show!--with me being the star!--well, that was way beyond what she could fathom.

So she came trompin' across the field, and when she saw the crowd of people circled round me, she knew this weren't no ordinary throwin' and catchin' game.

Our show was an eye-openin' phenomenon and you had to see it to believe it.

Now I can't tell you mama was amazed by what she seen.

Mama don't get amazed too often bein' on how much bad and good done already passed through her eyes.

But she was surprised.

Even she never imagined a snake glidin' through the sky on a wave of air, or parachutin' down from the clouds with a turquoise ring 'round their belly.

And, though she always knowed I was born with a gift, she never imagined how far me and grandma could go if'n we put our gifts together.

But more than the power of our gifts and the spectacle of snakes flyin' and twirlin' through the air was the crowds of people that came and watched with their eyes all glazed over and mesmerized like they was seein' some kind of miracle takin' place.

I guess the power of them mesmerizin' eyes was what finally got to mama.

See each mornin' she marched off to work, and each night she drug her beat body home, and the power of mesmerizin' eyes was somethin' she'd forgotten she had inside her.

And maybe the gift of bein' mesmerized was 'specially important to her on account of all the people she knew that owned the same dead eyes by the end of the day.

Or maybe it was 'cause it'd been so long since she saw their eyes sparkle with the ember of wonder.

Or 'cause she knowed that ember was what gave peoples hope of a better life.

Anyways, once mama saw what we'd created, she took over the "organization and management" of "Rainbo's Super-Spectacular Flyin' And Twirlin' Snake Show", and it weren't long 'fore she had our vacant field transformed into an amphi-theater.

She built benches and a raised stage in front of the oak tree which made us look larger than life.

And she created a refreshment stand and even a place to buy tickets for the show.

She set up a regular schedule of performances—two shows on Saturday and Sunday, and practices and trainin' "exhibitions" on Mondays, Wednesdays, and Fridays.

Even with a two dollar ticket price, people still poured in, and mama started thinkin' 'bout quittin' her job and takin' our show on the road.

'Course she knew with me in school and the Snake Clan livin' in the oak it weren't possible.

But she felt our gift of mesmer-izin' weren't reachin' 'enuff people.

Even if she gave out free tickets to all them people with beat eyes at work and down at the factories, and all them other

146

places she knowed where people's eyes were snuffed out by the hard life they lived, we weren't gonna reach enuff people to make the difference she wanted.

And that was the thing none of us knowed 'bout mama.

We all thought she was so preoc-cupied with makin' money and givin' us a better life, that she didn't care much 'bout other people.

But mama always wished she could make a difference in the world, and maybe change how things was always skewed in the wrong direction against the poor.

www.ingramcontent.com/pod-product-compliance
Lightning Source LLC
Chambersburg PA
CBHW022024170626
46808CB00003B/1050